THIS

SWEET PICKLES ®

BOOK
BELONGS TO

_____

In the Town of Sweet Pickles, the animals get into and out of pickles because of their all too human personality traits.

Each of the books in the *Sweet Pickles* series is about a different pickle.

This story is about putting things off... again.

Library of Congress Cataloging in Publication Data

Reinach, Jacquelyn.
    What a mess!
    (Sweet Pickles)
    SUMMARY: Goof Off Goose promises to clean up
the mess in her yard "tomorrow." A snow storm helps
her keep her promise to her neighbors.
    [1. Cleanliness — Fiction.   2. Animals — Fiction]
I. Hefter, Richard.   II. Perle, Ruth Lerner.
III. Title.   IV. Series: Sweet Pickles series.
PZ7.R2747Wf   [E]   80-22262
ISBN 0-937524-03-4

Published by Euphrosyne, Inc.

Sweet Pickles is the registered trademark of
Perle/Reinach/Hefter

Printed in the United States of America

Weekly Reader Books' Edition

Weekly Reader Books presents

WHAT A MESS!

Written by Jacquelyn Reinach
Illustrated by Richard Hefter
Edited by Ruth Lerner Perle

Euphrosyne Incorporated

Winter was coming. All the leaves were off the trees and the wind was getting chilly.

Everyone in the Town of Sweet Pickles was busy getting ready for the first snow ... except for Goof-Off Goose.

Responsible Rabbit was raking leaves.

Loving Lion was staking his rose trees for the winter.

Enormous Elephant was stacking her picnic furniture in the garage.

Zany Zebra was packing cans and bottles and tying newspapers.

Goose was lying in her hammock trying to take
her morning nap.
The neighborhood noises kept her awake.

"Hey!" cried Goose. "All this raking and staking and stacking and packing is spoiling my morning nap!"

"Your *yard* is spoiling the neighborhood!" cried Smarty Stork. He was coming by with the morning mail.

Stork put down his mail pouch and sniffed in disgust. "What a mess!" he said. "In my time, I have seen a lot of junk and skunky gunk. I have seen soggy garbage bags and filthy oily rags. I've seen rubbish and trash and broken glass. I've smelled sour milk and rotten tomatoes, moldy old cheese and wrinkled potatoes. But I have *never* seen a mess like this!"

"What mess?" yawned Goose. She sat up and stretched and looked around.

Goose's front yard was littered with empty ice cream cartons, old newspapers, cans, bottles, paper cups, a rubber tire and lots of other junk.

"Oh," said Goose. "I guess my yard *could* use a little fall clean-up, Stork. I'll do it first thing tomorrow. Tomorrow you won't see any junk in my yard, I promise!"

"Promises, promises!" groaned Stork. He flew off. Goose snuggled down and closed her eyes.

Just then there was a loud honking from a truck. It was Outraged Octopus collecting bundles for recycling.

"Hush!" said Goose. "Stop that awful honking! I'm trying to sleep!"

"Look who's talking about awful!" screamed Octopus. "Look at your yard. *That's* awful! What a mess!"

"Please don't yell," said Goose.

"I have a right to yell!" yelled Octopus. "Yesterday you said you would clean up your yard. You said you would bundle your newspapers and sort out your cans and bottles and have everything ready for pickup! Well?..."

"Well...I couldn't find any boxes to pack the stuff in," said Goose.

Octopus tossed some empty boxes off the truck. "Here!" she shouted. "Take these and fill them up! Now you have no excuse, Goose!"

Octopus drove off.

"Okay," called Goose. "Tomorrow you won't see any junk in my yard. I promise!"

Goose looked around. "I guess I'll get started tomorrow," she sighed. "If only I knew what to do first!"

"If I were you, Goose," called Rabbit from next door, "I would make a careful list of everything I had to do."

"Yes," said Goose. "And then?"

"And then," shouted Rabbit, "DO IT!"

"Oh!" said Goose. "That's a good idea. I'll make a list of everything I'm going to do tomorrow...as soon as I find a pencil."

"Tomorrow you won't see any junk in my yard," promised Goose. Then she went into the house.

That evening, Goose sat down to make a list. She wrote down the first thing: CLEAN UP THE MESS. Then she got tired and fell asleep.

During the night, it got colder and colder. The wind howled and it began to snow.

It snowed harder and harder. It snowed on the ice cream cartons. It snowed on the newspapers. It snowed on the cans and the bottles and the paper cups. Snow covered all the junk in Goose's yard.

When Goose woke up the next morning, she looked at her list. "Oh," she yawned. "Today is the day I should clean up the yard. I promised the junk would be gone."

Then Goose looked out the window. "Well, what do you know? Snow!" she smiled. She stuck her head out to have a better look.

A thick blanket of white snow covered her entire front yard. Everything looked clean and sparkling in the sunlight.

"Imagine that!" said Goose with a little twinkle in her eye. "You can't see any junk in my yard! The snow has kept my promise!"

Goose closed the window gently and went back to bed.

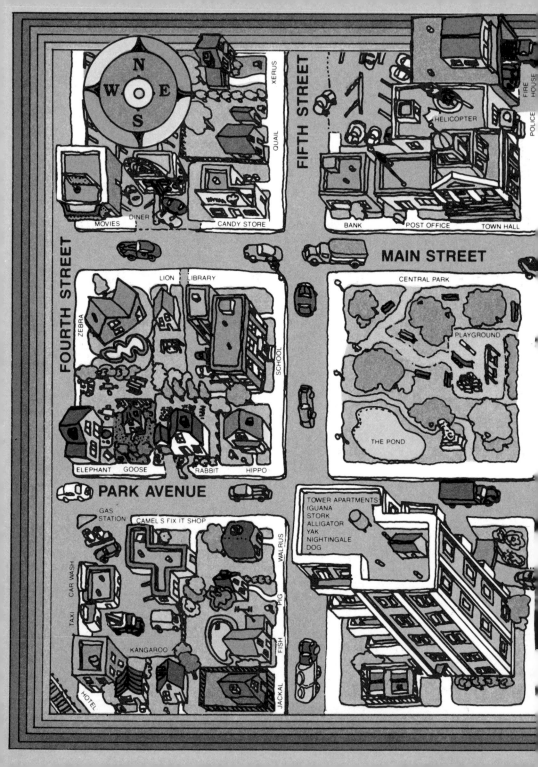